# Donte

**Obsidian Mechanics, Volume 1**

S L Davies

Published by S L Davies, 2022.

DONTE

**First edition. September 13, 2022.**



ISBN: 979-8215850435

Written by S L Davies.

S avannah

"Oh, my word, March, he is so beautiful. He is like a complete mix of Bear and Ivy," I gushed as I looked down into the face of my newest nephew, Hiro. March had, had so much trouble keeping a pregnancy. He'd had so many miscarriages, and with every miscarriage, his depression gripped him harder. But now, he had three beautiful children. All strong and healthy.

"He is our last one," March said with a sigh.

I nodded and reached out my hand to link my fingers with my brothers. "I know. I'm sorry, March."

March shrugged his shoulders. "I keep thinking how I should be looking at the good side; I've three healthy and happy children. But I feel like this dark cloud surrounds me, pointing out that I'd only ever have three children."

"Have you told Asher and your doctor how you feel?"

March bit into his bottom lip and shook his head.

"You need to, March. You might need a little bit of help with your mental health. That is nothing to be ashamed of."

Tears welled up in March's eyes. He angrily swiped at them with the back of his hand. "I'm so fucking sick of crying," he growled.

"March," I started. Worry crept into me. Having a baby should be a happy event, but I could see March wasn't feeling it. I also knew that if I didn't speak to him before our sisters got here, they would be all over him, making everything worse.

March sighed. "I know. I don't understand what is wrong with me. I love Hiro and all my children, but I just don't feel happy. I don't want to do the things that Hiro needs. I can't even face it when he starts crying. Then I feel like shit because I'm supposed to be his Papa and enjoy doing it all."

I frowned and nodded my head. "You need to speak to Asher and your doctor about this March. You're right. You shouldn't be feeling like this; it sounds like depression to me. But I'm not a doctor. Please tell me you will talk to Asher."

"Talk to me about what?" Asher asked as he walked into the living room.

March looked up and sighed before looking away. Asher frowned and watched March; I could see that he was trying to figure out what was happening. I wondered how long this had been going on for. This wasn't just affecting March and his relationship with his children; it potentially could destroy his mateship.

"March isn't coping," I exclaimed.

March sneered, and I knew he'd be pissed with me for letting Asher in, but I couldn't sit back and watch my brother sink into his depression further. I needed to do something. Not just for March's sake but the children too.

Asher nodded his head. "Yeah, I'd gathered that you were struggling, baby, but what are you struggling with?"

March sighed, and when he looked up, his eyes were wet with tears. "Everything. I'm struggling with it all. I don't want to be a Papa anymore. I don't want to be a mate. I don't want to do any of it; I want to go to bed and never climb out again."

My eyes widened, but when I looked at Asher, his face was stoic; I could tell from his eyes that what March said stung, but he was also mature enough to see past it.

"How long have you felt this way?" Asher asked quietly.

March shrugged his shoulders. "Since I had Hiro and the doctors told me my body wouldn't cope with children anymore. When the doctors started telling me that I would need to have my birth sac removed." Tears started tearing down March's cheeks, and the hurt he was feeling threaded his voice.

"Oh, sweet boy," Asher said as he walked towards March and gathered him up in his arms. "Why didn't you tell me?"

"I didn't want to put it all on you. Asher, you have already do so much, between running the club and the time you spend helping with Bear and Ivy. I didn't want to add this on to you as well."

"March, that is what I'm here for. I'm your partner. I'm here to pick you up when you aren't strong enough. Baby, I love you. You never have to burden this on your own."

Tears prickled in my eyes at the beauty of the moment. I thought about Donte and wondered whether he would ever be the same towards me. I smiled as I realized that Donte was the same. He might not have grown up in the same loving household that Asher Rigby did, but he still had worked out how to show his love.

"I will go to the doctors," March said with a sigh.

"I'll make an appointment," Asher responded.

"In the meantime, I'm going to stay and help you care for the children. You aren't alone in this March," I said. "Hell, you've got nineteen sisters willing to help you. Not to mention all the Rigby's. The club and the Devil's Advocates. You've got a lot of people who would be willing to share some of the burdens."

March breathed in deeply and looked over at me with a small smile. "Thank you, Savannah. I love you."

I leaned over and kissed my brother's cheek. "I love you too."

# Chapter One

D onte

"Alright, what have we got on," Boden asked as he strode into the shop of Obsidian Mechanics. I glanced down the list I had in my hand and looked back at the warlock.

"We've got Mrs. Newton's brakes to finish; Atticus is working on the ford over there. I've got a service to do on the Mazda, and I know that Lynx was bringing in a couple of bikes with Jai from the Devil's Advocates to get looked at. From what Jai told me this morning, they are rattling. He said they are going 'rattle, rattle, bing, bang.' Whatever the hell that means."

Boden chuckled. We were all well versed in Jai's technical talk now that we went with the flow, but when I'd first met the MC member, I wasn't sure how to take him. In fact, since meeting all the Devil's Advocates and everyone around Lalbert, I'd changed so much.

I fucking hated the idea of my brother-in-law being mated to Rigby. I never thought I'd see the day I would be working for one, in the MC of another and calling them all my brothers. I grew up rough. We never had any money. Dad and Papa pissed most of it away; whatever was left usually went to paying other people they'd borrowed money from throughout the week.

Then when they ran out of booze, that was when the violence started. I was usually their punching bag. It caused a real chip on my shoulder. When I met Asher for the first time, and he just oozed wealth, I instantly hated him. It didn't take long for the bear shifter to put me back in my place, though. He offered me a job in Lalbert with Obsidian Mechanics; technically, it belonged to Asher's brother Obsidian, but Asher owned a stake in the business so he could offer me a job.

After a few harsh words from my mate Savannah, I pulled my head out of my ass and agreed to take on the job. We were also given a place to live on one of the Devil's Advocates compounds. At first, I wondered if we were just a Rigby family charity case. But it didn't take long before I realized they were genuine and a fantastic family. Since then, I've never looked back.

I didn't tell Dad and Papa I was leaving Lancaster. I just up and left. Not that they've ever tried to contact me. As far as Dad and Papa were concerned, I was dead to them when I mated with Savannah. They didn't hold much value in a family unit.

It shouldn't surprise me when I looked at where they came from. My Papa was born in a wolf pack. One of the biggest in Australia. The Wild Claw Pack. My Papa's father was the alpha of the pack; from everything Papa ever said of my grandfather, he hated omegas. Even the one that he was mated to. When Papa was born an omega, the moment he turned eighteen, he was outcasted from the pack.

I never knew how real the story was or if Papa had done something to cause him to be kicked out, but that was the story Papa told me. From there, he moved to Lancaster, where he met my Dad.

Dad was different. He wasn't raised in a pack like Papa. He had always been rogue. His father was a wolf shifter, but his mother was a vampire. Generally, those that came from more than one species weren't welcomed into packs. I didn't know much about Dad's upbringing and had never met my grandparents from either parent. When I asked Dad about them, I usually got slapped or punched, so I quickly learned that it was a subject not to be spoken about.

The day I met Savannah was the happiest day of my life. She was my everything. The only thing that could have made our life better was if Savannah was able to get pregnant. It wasn't like we weren't trying. But no matter how many doctors told us there was no reason she couldn't get pregnant and how many healers we went to, Savannah and I never had a child.

I knew it hurt Savannah, the one thing she desperately wanted, and I felt like a complete failure that I couldn't give her a baby. Doctors had checked us both over and said that we were fine. We'd gone to the witch coven here in Lalbert, and they said they couldn't find any reason why we weren't falling pregnant. We even asked Arcadia, the dragon shifter that worked with the AJE authority, and she couldn't find the problem.

I might've given up on having children somewhere inside me, but Savannah was much more positive than me. She lived in the hope that maybe one day, we would be blessed. I hoped so. But I was doubtful.

I sighed and shook my head, washing away the depressing thoughts that surrounded me when I thought about the babies and my family. I glanced over at the Mazda and sucked in a deep breath. There was work to be done. Everyone was hard at it. Obsidian was back at work now that Pitt and Juniper were healed after their traumatic birth. Now it was back to business as usual.

# Chapter Two

S able
"We found him," I said as I ran into the alpha house on the pack lands. Connell gasped and looked up from the paper he was scouring.

"I'm hoping you are talking about my son," Connell growled. I rolled my eyes at the old bastard. Of course, I was talking about his son. We have searched for him for the last twenty-seven years since Serge and Kragen took him from the pack.

"He grew up in a town called Lancaster. Serge and Kragen are still there," I explained.

Connell leaned forward, looking more interested. The baby had disappeared straight from his crib the first night after birth. It was quickly discovered that the one responsible for his abduction had been Serge. Connell's brother. Unfortunately, during the kidnapping, Connell lost his son and his mate. Harley had taken her life only months later. It had almost destroyed the pack. Connell sunk into a depression determined to find his son; as the years went on, we thought all hope was lost.

I wasn't born when Connell's son was taken. The baby hadn't even been named yet. Our pack didn't name our children until the first full moon after their birth. When the moon was at its highest, goddess Selene spoke to the parents. It was then that the child would be named. That meant searching for the child was like searching for a needle in a haystack.

Over the years, many had taken on the role of trying to find the son, Serge or Kragen, but every lead we had, fell short. There seemed to be no trace of them until recently. It was just by chance that Kragen's name came up in a google search. He'd been charged with assault on a man in the town of Lancaster.

"What do we know?" Connell asked as he sent a text, which I knew would be to the other three alphas of the pack, Ward, Fenris, and

Herrick. Our group was large; Wild Claw was known over Victoria, Australia, for their size and ferocity. We weren't ferocious. We protected what was ours. Hidden in the valley of Trentham, we tended to keep to ourselves. But the times we had to come into town, people gave us a wide berth. It probably had to do with the fact that most of the alphas looked like they had just stepped straight out of a Vikings ship. But really, they were big softies.

"Kragen and Serge are in a small town called Lancaster, as I said. It is a small farming community of about one thousand people. I could tell from census records that they had been there all the child's life. Lancaster is up in the northern part of Victoria. I hadn't heard of it before this morning."

Connell nodded his head. "Is my son still there?"

I shook my head as the other alphas walked into the room. "No. He is in the next town over. His name is Donte. He is mated to a spider shifter, Savannah, and is part of an MC called the Devil's Advocates. He is a mechanic and works for Obsidian Mechanics in Lalbert."

Connell frowned and glanced over at Fenris. "Do you know the MC?"

Fenris nodded his head. "Yeah. I've never met them, but I've heard of them. From what I know, they are celebrated; they've done a shit ton of work in helping to break down breeding facilities. And they are involved in this war that we've heard rumors of."

Connell hummed. The war, as far as we knew, was still just a rumor. There was talk that it was supposed to take place somewhere in Victoria and that there was a Nephilim who was going to rise to enslave not only humans but supernaturals too. I hadn't thought much, but the idea that someone might be given that much power was terrifying.

"What do you want to do?" Ward asked Connell.

"Have you been able to make contact with Donte?" Connell asked me.

I shook my head. "No. We've been using Mars to help find him. As soon as I found Kragen and Serge, I had Mars scry and find Donte."

Connell nodded his head. "Does he look happy? Healthy?"

I smiled and nodded. "He does. He seems very happy with the Devil's Advocates and in love with his mate Savannah."

Connell sighed before looking over at the other alphas. "What do you think? This will completely disrupt his entire life. Do we go?"

"You have been searching for your son for the last twenty-seven years. Not just for your sake but for Harley's memory, we need to search him out and tell him the truth," Fenris said.

I understood Fenris's anger. It was his sister, Harley, that had died as a result of Donte's abduction. She'd died with a broken heart, never knowing where her son was or whether he was alive or dead.

"If nothing else, I think it's time to make Kragen and Serge pay for what they did," Ward growled.

I nodded my head. "I want to come too," I demanded. I had spent most of my life helping my father find Serge and Kragen. I wanted to see it through the end.

"You've raised a damned shield maiden," Connell laughed as he looked over at my father, Herrick.

Dad chuckled and rolled his eyes. "More like her mother than I'm willing to admit."

I sighed with a smile on my face. My mother was a wonderful woman. Strong and forever remembered. She died when I was thirteen years old. They forget to tell you when you are supernatural that you aren't indestructible. I found that out when I found my mother dead, at the bottom of the stairs. The doctors said she'd had a stroke. But none of that mattered to me; all it meant was I would have to bury my Mama and never see that beautiful smile or feel her warm hug again.

"Alright, let's pack and get ready to go to Lancaster. We will decide what to do about Donte once we are done dealing with Serge and Kragen," Connell said as he stood from his chair.

"Who will look after the pack while we are gone?" Dad asked.

Connell hummed. "I think it's time for Lobo to take on more, no?"

Herrick chuckled. "The boy will love that."

Connell smiled and nodded his head. My brother Lobo had been desperate to become one of the alpha leaders. He was twenty-eight years old and was set to take over once our father retired from his position. But my dad was still a young man. Now Lobo was going to get his chance. I knew that the pack would be left safe; Lobo was a good man; he was fair and had been trained as an alpha.

# Chapter Three

Savannah
"Fuck, you are good at that," Donte groaned as he placed his arms up under his head. I giggled as I licked my tongue along the shaft of his cock, all the way to the head. "Babe, I'm gonna cum if you keep doing that."

I giggled again as I climbed the bed. I'd had heat only a week earlier and hoped like crazy I'd be pregnant. It was my same wish, with every heat cycle. But again, there was no pregnancy. You'd think I'd give up after a while, but I couldn't.

Focusing back on Donte, who was watching me with hooded lids. No matter how old we got, that man never got any less sexy. His dark hair and eyes matched the stubble on his chin. The tattoos I took a great time licking and kissing all over his body. I slipped my leg over his hips to straddle him before grinding my pussy down along his shaft.

Donte hissed and grasped hold of my hips. He looked like he wasn't sure whether he wanted to stop me or guide my movements. With a smile, I lifted my hips so that the head of his cock sat at my entrance before slowly sliding down. I moaned as his dick stretched me out. God, I could never get sick of this man's cock.

Rocking back and forth, I ground down into him, tossing my head back as I let the pleasure envelop me and wash over my body. Donte's fingers roamed over my stomach up to my chest before taking my nipples between his thumb and finger, squeezing them and making them tighter than they already were. The slight sting added to my pleasure as I rode him with lust.

Our moans mingled, and I felt my orgasm right on the precipice. I knew that Donte was close. I could feel his knot starting to form and knew that the minute it locked, I would be sent hurtling into the most erotic pleasure I'd ever experienced. Just a few more thrusts. And there, Donte's knot locked in place, and I cried out as it hit on my gspot. I clawed into my mate's chest as I felt his cock throb inside me. His roar sounded around me as he filled me full of cum.

Slowly our breathing returned to normal, and I settled into Donte's chest. Closing my eyes, I listened to his heartbeat return to normal.

"I love you," I said quietly.

Donte's fingers stroked up and down my back, and he kissed my hair. "I love you too, baby. Is everything alright?"

I sighed. Donte knew how much it hurt every heat cycle when I wouldn't fall pregnant. Watching the omegas around us at the compounds falling pregnant and having healthy children was getting harder and harder. My family had nineteen siblings, all popping out children, left, right and center. Yet I still couldn't have a baby.

"I just want one of our own," I said quietly as I felt the sting of tears burn at my eyes.

"I know, baby. I just wish there was something I could do to change it. I feel like we've exhausted every avenue."

It was true. We had. Between doctors and mysticals, there wasn't much left. We'd tried all sorts of healing, we'd both undergone so many tests to try and find out why we couldn't fall pregnant, but no one had any answers for me. And every heat cycle, I would leave disappointed when I found I wasn't pregnant. Again.

I sighed. "It's alright. Maybe we could investigate adoption. I know Anghus and Bacchus said that there were still some babies from the Hunter Island facility they shut down that needed permanent homes."

Donte smiled up at me and nodded his head. "If you want to do that, then, of course, we can do that."

"Do you think we would make good parents?"

Donte winced. He'd come from a horrible home. His fathers were bastards who didn't deserve the title of father. They were incredibly abusive. The day I met Donte; he was covered in bruises. I thought he'd got into a fight at school, which he was prepared to let me believe, had it not been for Serge finding him in the street and walloping him right there and then. After that, he couldn't hide it from me. But it didn't matter so much then. Once we were mated, we were able to move away. Now that we lived in Lalbert, we didn't see Serge or Kragen anymore. I was aware Donte hadn't even heard from them since we left.

Good riddance to them, I felt. But I knew that it still stung Donte.

"You will be a wonderful mother. Me. I don't know."

I shook my head. "Donte, you will be a great Papa. I know you would be. You are so good with all the nephews and nieces."

"Speaking of which, when is it our turn to look after Bear, Ivy, and Hiro again?"

I smiled and sighed. I loved all my nephews and nieces, but I had a particular soft spot for my brothers' children. There was something magical about them. Something that made them different.

"Tomorrow afternoon. Asher has some work he needs to get done. I promised I'd go over and pick them up after lunch. But I told him that he and March should go and spend a dirty afternoon at the club," I giggled when Donte gagged.

"I do not want to think of your brother and what they do at that club."

I snorted. "They don't have three babies by just showering together."

Donte groaned. "God, stop, please, for the love of all that is holy, don't do that to my ears."

I snorted again and shook my head. "You are so damned dramatic."

Donte flashed me that smile that always made me melt before he leaned forward and pressed his lips against mine. I groaned and rocked my hips, feeling his knot having gone down slightly, but enough to leave pressure inside me.

"Round two?" Donte asked.

Giggling, I nodded my head. "Round two," I agreed.

# Chapter Four

D<sup>onte</sup>

"Fucking hell," I grunted as I slammed my head into the car's underside as my phone started to buzz in my pocket. I wrestled it out and looked down at the ID. Rolling my eyes, I ignored the call yet again. I didn't know what was happening, but my Papa had been trying to ring me all morning. I thought he'd get the idea that I wasn't about to answer after the fourth rejected call, but instead, he kept ringing.

I was just about to put my phone back in my pocket when it started ringing again. "Fucking what?" I snapped as I answered the call.

"Woah, who pissed in your cornflakes?" Jai's voice cackled on the other end.

"Sorry, man, I thought it was my Papa calling again," I sighed. I slid out from beneath the car and sat up on the trolley.

"Yeah, that's what I was calling you about. He had just rocked up at the secondary compound; Savannah rang panicked; she had the kids there. Thankfully Kenji was there and could stop your Papa from breaking down the door."

"Shit, is Sav and the kids alright?" I asked; worry circled my stomach. I wondered briefly where my Dad was.

"Yeah, they are fine. She is a little shaken up, but Mama and Papa are there with her now. Papa won't let anyone in until you get back."

"Thanks, man," I said as I scrubbed my hands over my face. I glanced at the clock; it was barely lunchtime. Obsidian came running into the shop just as I ended the call with Jai.

"Was that Jai?" he asked, sounding panicked.

"Yeah. You heard about my Papa then?"

Obsidian nodded his head. "Anghus is going to meet you back at the compound. He wants to make sure that you are safe."

"Thanks, man," I said with a sigh as I stood from the trolley. "I'm sorry that my family fuckery has come here."

Obsidian took hold of my arm and squeezed. "You and Savannah are family. Whatever you need, we are here for you guys. Take it easy, and I know that you will be safe with Anghus there."

I smiled and nodded my head. Walking out of the shop, I headed for my bike. Kicking it to life, I sped out of the shop and towards the secondary compound where Savannah and I lived. My mind was spinning with what the hell Papa could possibly want. Part of me hoped that maybe he wanted to make amends, but my critical mind knew he wasn't. He probably got himself in trouble and needed someone to bail him out. I still wondered where Dad was.

I pulled into the compound and stopped at the guard house, where I saw Anghus, Lynx, and Israel's bikes. I breathed out a breath of relief. At least I had backup. It was stupid to be still scared of my fathers, but it was something left over from my childhood. I'd taken enough beatings to create so much fear in me.

I killed the engine on my bike and climbed off. Shaking off the nerves, I wiped my hands on my pants and walked toward the guard house. Anghus met me at the door with a smile, but his eyes said something different.

"What's he want?" I asked. I couldn't mistake the fear that trembled in my voice.

"Donte, your Dad. He was killed. By the Wild Claw Pack."

I frowned and shook my head. That made no sense. I knew they'd kicked Papa out for being an omega, but I didn't understand why they would come to Lancaster to kill Dad. From what I'd known about the Wild Claw Pack, they had pack lands in the hills of Trentham and Daylesford. They kept to themselves and didn't leave the area.

I breathed in deeply and nodded my head. Passing by Anghus, I moved into the guard house. Papa sat on a chair surrounded by the Devil's Advocates. He looked up at me with red eyes.

"They killed him, son," Papa said as he stood and wobbled towards me. I could smell the alcohol before he draped his body over mine in an awkward hug.

"Why?" I asked.

Papa stumbled backward and crashed back down into the chair he'd vacated. "They always hated me," Papa said. "They probably were always hunting us. And finally, they found us."

I frowned and shook my head. "I don't understand, Papa. The Wild Claw Pack are five hours away from us; why would they have been hunting you down all this time if they kicked you out for being an omega? None of it makes sense. What really is going on here?"

Papa shrugged his shoulders and looked up at me with pitiful eyes. But there was something in that look that was deceitful. I didn't know how I knew. But I could tell that he was lying. There was more to the story.

I said nothing but turned and walked away. I exited the guardhouse and went to my bike; pulling out my cigarettes, I lit one up, inhaling deep.

"What are you thinking?" Israel asked.

"He's full of shit. There is a reason they killed Dad."

"Yeah," Israel replied as he leaned against his bike. "There is something shady going on."

I nodded my head. "I don't want him anywhere near Savannah or the kids. I don't trust him. He is an evil son of a bitch. And to be honest, I'm glad Dad is dead."

Israel winced but nodded his head. "I get it, man. I get it."

I sighed and scrubbed my hands up over my face. I didn't know what to do. If the Wild Claw Pack really were hunting Dad and Papa down, then they would no doubt follow Papa here, which means that there was a chance that the omegas would be in danger.

"We need to get him away from here," I said. "If he is telling the truth, the omegas are in danger."

Israel nodded his head. "I agree. Anghus and Lynx are currently working on finding him somewhere to stay. But I think we are going to have to watch him."

Suddenly the roar of engines filled the air.

"Shit, that's not us," Anghus said.

"Fuck," I growled.

Bikes pulled into the compound and stopped. I stood beside Anghus, Lynx, Israel, and Kenji as four men and one woman climbed from their bikes.

"Donte?" one of the men asked. He looked like he could have quickly passed as a Viking. His hair was shaved at the sides, and the top was braided. I lifted my nose and breathed in his scent, all wolf shifter, but there was another scent that surrounded him. One that was familiar.

"Yeah," I said, stepping forward.

"Where is Serge?" he asked.

"Who are you?"

"I'm Connell Wild, the alpha of the Wild Claw Pack. Do you know who I am?"

"I know of you. I know of your pack; I want to know what you want with my father?"

Connell sneered and shook his head. "He isn't your father," he spat.

My eyes widened, and I gasped.

"He's lying," Papa roared as he came out of the guardhouse. "He's lying."

I looked over at Papa, who appeared wild with wide eyes and veins bulging. I looked back at the Devil's Advocates that surrounded me. I didn't know what to make of what was going on. The Wild Claw Pack hadn't moved. They hadn't said anything about killing Papa; they just stood staring.

"Did you kill my father?" I asked.

Connell nodded his head. "I killed Kragen, yes."

"Why?"

"As I said, he is not your father. What do you know of where you came from?"

"Shut the fuck up, Connell," Papa snarled.

Connell turned on my Papa and curled his lip. "No, brother, you shut the fuck up. You are fucking lucky I haven't killed you right now."

Papa's eyes widened, and he stumbled backward into Kenji. I looked between Papa and Connell. *Brother?*

"I think someone needs to explain; what the fuck is going on?" I spat.

Connell nodded his head. "You are my son. You were taken from my mate and me on your second day on earth. You were taken by my brother Serge and his mate Kragen. They couldn't have their own children, so they decided to take mine." The disgust threaded through Connell's voice hit me in the chest and took my breath away.

"Is that true?" I asked with wide eyes as I turned back to Papa or Serge.

Papa wouldn't look at me. He said nothing as he kept his face to the ground.

"Fuck you," I spat. "Fuck you, you cunt. You're piece of shit." I roared as I ran towards Papa and balled my hand into a fist, letting it fly into his nose.

Papa grunted as his head snapped back. All I could see was red as I reigned blows down into the man, I'd believed to be my father. A man that had beaten me every day of my childhood. A man that had treated me so horribly that I was sure he hated me. A man that wasn't even supposed to have me.

"How the fuck could you? You fucking beat me. You had me raped. You had me beaten. I was just some fucking ass for you to sell. And I wasn't even fucking yours," I spat in between punches.

When I felt Anghus pull me off him and into his arms, I was heaving great gulping breaths. Savannah's scent surrounded me, and tears fell as I pulled my mate into my arms. I couldn't look at Serge. I couldn't face the man that had taken me.

"I need to go, baby," I said.

"I'm coming with you," she said as I climbed onto my bike. She climbed on the back, and I brought it to life; without another word, I turned the bike out of the compound and tore out to the road. I didn't know where I was going, but I needed to get away. I couldn't face any of this.

# Chapter Five

S able
Killing Kragen had been easy. The alpha had cowered like a fucking dog. He cried and pleaded with Connell not to kill him, but it was too late. We knew his fate. The man had taken the heir to the Wild Claw Pack throne. He'd hidden him away for twenty-seven years. His sentence was always going to be death.

We hadn't counted that Serge would skulk away and escape. By the time Mars had found him, he was already in Lalbert at one of the Devil's Advocates compounds. I watched in shock as Donte had beaten the man he thought was a father. A man that apparently had treated him terribly. It just made my anger stronger.

Nothing was recognizable of Serge after Donte had finished with him. He was dead. Connell glared down at the omega shifter. His own brother. Disgust couldn't even describe how I felt about Serge and Kragen.

"Kenji, can you organize his body to be taken away? I'd rather not have the omegas see this. We may need to let Kade know what has happened," a man said, who I discovered was Anghus, the president of the Devil's Advocates.

He had to be one of the most enormous people I'd ever seen. He stood nearly seven feet and was just as broad across the shoulders and full of muscle. From his scent, I could tell he was a gargoyle.

The man Anghus had spoken to nodded and lifted his phone to his ear before he started giving directions to get Serge's body removed. I didn't care what happened to it. I couldn't put my finger on what it was I was feeling. But there had been something about Donte. It was in the way his scent lingered, and when his mate had arrived, the smell had doubled.

"Right, I think we all need to have a talk," Anghus said. "Follow us; we will head out to the main compound. This one is mostly filled with omegas that have been through enough shit and don't really trust strangers very well."

Connell nodded his head and silently walked back to his bike. I turned and followed, climbing onto my bike; we gunned them to life and took off towards wherever Anghus was taking us. I had to trust that we were safe; Connell would not have allowed us to go if we weren't.

After a short ride, we pulled up through what looked like a forest from the outside. But on the inside was nothing short of gorgeous. It was very much like the pack lands back home. There were houses and buildings dotted throughout the property, lined with forest. I could just envision having the opportunity to run through the woods.

Once we pulled up to a large house, I climbed off my bike and stood beside my father. There was something magical about the place. I couldn't explain it. But there was a strong power that surged through me. I'd never felt anything like it.

"Do you feel that?" I asked.

Dad nodded his head. "It's powerful. The land, but the people too."

"Yeah," I agreed.

Anghus, who must have heard us smiled. "This land is built on fae lines of old. This town is magical, but this piece of property is the epicenter. The people here are prophesied to be the most powerful of this generation. They will be integral in the war that is coming."

I frowned and nodded my head. "The war is real?"

Anghus nodded. "Yes. It's coming sooner than what we realize."

Connell hummed in his throat. "And it will be fought here, yes?"

Anghus nodded again. "That's right. You know about the war?"

"I did a little bit of research before we came. I wanted to know about the Devil's Advocates. I wanted to know where my son was and who he was involved with," Connell replied.

Anghus smiled. "That's fair enough; I would do the same. Please, come in; I think we have a lot to talk about. Donte will come here once he cools down a bit."

Connell nodded, and we followed Anghus up the stairs into the large house. It was just as beautiful inside. Anghus led us into a vast living room where an omega was sitting holding a baby. The omega glanced up with a smile, and I instantly recognized that he was Anghus's mate.

"This is my mate Joachim and our daughter Canea. Sweetheart, these are members of the Wild Claw Pack," Anghus introduced.

"It's lovely to meet you all," Joachim answered.

"And you," Connell replied. "My name is Connell; this is Herrick, Fenris, Ward, and Sable."

Suddenly the door to the front of the house opened and closed before another large man came in.

"Kenji rang. Are you all okay?" the man asked.

Anghus smiled and leaned over, kissing the man briefly on the lips. "We are fine. This is my other mate, Bacchus. He works for the AJE authority. These are the alphas of the Wild Claw Pack."

"I don't understand what is going on?" Bacchus said with a shake of his head.

"Let's sit and talk," Anghus said with a smile as he waved his hand over the seats.

Joachim stood before handing the baby to Bacchus. "I'll go and get us some coffee."

I smiled at Joachim. "Would you like a hand?"

Joachim waved his hand and shook his head. "All good. All that testosterone gets a bit much for me," he giggled.

I grinned and turned my attention back to the Devil's Advocates members.

"This is Lynx, our VP, and Israel, our sergeant at arms," Anghus introduced. "No doubt the other inner members will roam in and out at some stage as the news filters through. What is your story?"

Connell sighed and ran his hands up over his face. "As you are now aware, Serge was my brother. He and Kragen were never able to have children; it didn't matter how much they tried and how many healers they went to, they could never conceive. Serge was older than me and was jealous when I mated with my late mate. Donte's mother. Harley. She was able to conceive on our mating, and six months later, Donte arrived. Although, his name wasn't Donte. We don't name our children until the full moon of their first month. The day after he was born, Serge and Kragen visited; they said they wanted to give Harley a chance to nap. I was out with pack business. I got a frantic call; Harley was screaming. My brother and his mate had taken our son."

"Shit," Lynx spat and shook his head. "I can only imagine the pain that caused."

Connell nodded his head. "A lot. I searched everywhere. But I don't know how they managed to evade me. I couldn't find them. Then six months after the kidnapping, Harley, she just couldn't take it anymore," Connell's voice hitched, and his tears welled in his eyes. "She committed suicide."

"Fuck, I'm sorry," Israel said.

Connell nodded. "I vowed that I would never give up looking for my son. It didn't matter how old or long it took; I would find him. Then yesterday, it was Sable that announced she'd found him."

The Devil's Advocates members turned their attention to me, and my cheeks blushed as I shrugged my shoulders. "Kragen's name came up in a google search that I had constantly run for them. He had been charged with assault; it gave away where he was."

Anghus smiled and nodded his head. "Donte, sorry, what did you want to call him?"

Connell smiled and sighed. "His name would have been decided by the goddess, but now that he has spent so long known as Donte, then that is what I'll call him. Unless he wants to change it."

Anghus nodded his head. "He had a rough life."

"Then I'm not sad they are dead."

Anghus nodded again as Joachim brought a tray of coffee mugs to hand out.

# Chapter Six

S avannah

I could feel the anger rolling off Donte as we rode out of Lalbert and towards Lancaster. I wasn't sure where we were headed, but I would follow Donte anywhere. I loved him. He was my mate. I still wasn't entirely up to speed with what happened. All I knew was one minute I was looking after March's children, and the next, Serge was pounding down the door and trying to get in.

I'd called Anghus and Obsidian to try and get a hold of Donte because every time I tried to ring him, the phone would be busy. Jantzen told me that was because Serge was trying to call Donte. The children were terrified and cowered against me as we watched the door being kicked. I was never so grateful for the locks that Anghus had installed. They held up well.

After what felt like forever, finally, I could hear Serge being dragged away. After that, Gwen and Jantzen came with their daughter Amity who took Bear and Ivy into her arms and held them. Such a sweet girl, she was able to settle Ivy down, who was crying steady tears, while Bear got the same look Asher did when he was angry. His brow was furrowed, and he looked like he would do anything to protect his siblings.

Once I got a text from Anghus that they had arrived, I left Bear, Ivy, and Hiro with Gwen and Jantzen, while I went to look for Donte. I'd just found him when I saw him punching the life out of Serge. Looking down at his Papa's body, I saw he was dead. There was nothing left but a bloody husk of a body.

Part of me felt like I should feel bad, but I didn't care. I hated the man for the way he'd treated Donte. I was sure I didn't know Donte's entire story; I was sure there were parts he left out, but I knew that whatever the rest of the story was, it was awful.

Slowly Donte pulled up in front of the house that he'd grown up in. It was probably a house that should have been condemned. The lawns were overgrown, the weatherboards looked like they needed a good painting, and the house leaned slightly.

Donte killed the engine on the bike and breathed out a harsh breath. I stroked my hands up and down his back as we stared at the house.

"They aren't my fathers," he said quietly.

I frowned. "How did you find that out?"

"Those people that were there, the Wild Claw Pack, one of them was my father." I hissed and shook my head. Donte scoffed out a laugh and sighed. "All the bullshit Serge told me growing up that the Wild Claw Pack had kicked him out because he was an omega. It was all a lie. He'd kidnapped me as a baby along with Kragen."

I continued to stroke my hands up and down Donte's back as I leaned forward and kissed his shoulder.

"He's probably in there dead," Donte sighed.

"Kragen?"

"Yeah," he replied before turning on the bike to face me. "Do you think I'm bad that I just don't care? I mean fuck, I killed Serge." Donte looked down at his fists, which were cracked and covered in blood.

I used Donte's shoulder to help me to climb from the bike and stood beside him. Reaching out, I cupped Donte's cheeks in my hands.

"Never would I think you were bad for not caring about those pieces of shit. What they did to you growing up, you're a better person than I am to let them have lived at all."

Donte smiled sadly at me. "I don't know how I feel, to be honest. I'm so overwhelmed. If what Connell said was true, he is my father. I should have been raised in the Wild Claw Pack. But instead, I was raised by my uncle and his mate, who abused me every day of my life. Why would they take me if they hated me?"

I sighed and shook my head. "I don't know, baby. I'm sorry I don't have the answers for you. I wish I did. Do you want to get to know Connell?"

Donte shrugged. "I don't know. Part of me does. When I think about everything, part of me is excited at the prospect of learning that I have a father. He might've loved me so much that he searched for me for twenty-seven years. But then the other part of me is scared. I'm scared I'd be too different from Connell because of my life so far, and he would hate me. I mean, I'm not exactly the easiest person to get to know."

I smiled. "I don't know; you let me in."

"That's because you were my mate, and I fell in love with you the moment I laid eyes on you."

I giggled and blushed. No matter how often he told me things like that, it always had the same effect.

"What do you want to do about Kragen?"

Donte breathed in deeply before slowly letting it out. "I suppose we should let Kade know. I don't know what that will mean for Connell, though."

Technically, Connell murdered Kragen and Donte murdered Serge. I bit into my bottom lip as I thought about what Donte said. I hoped that Kade would look at it differently as being pack business. But I wasn't too sure.

"Do you want to go back to the compound and talk to Anghus? He will probably be able to tell us more," I suggested.

Donte scrubbed his hand down over his face and nodded his head. "Yeah. I'm tempted to light a match and just let it all burn to the ground."

A black car slowed before stopping out the front of the house, and I recognized Pax and Coltrane climbing out of the front seats.

"Hey, man," Coltrane said as he came over to where we stood. "Do you know if Kragen is still inside?"

Donte shook his head. "No. I haven't been in."

Coltrane nodded and walked towards the front of the house. We could see that the front door had been kicked in. I watched as Coltrane entered the house before he exited quickly.

"Yup, he is," Coltrane said with a sigh.

"What is going to happen?" I asked.

"We were sent here by Kade. It's a tricky situation because this didn't happen on pack lands, so he has to do some work to get it to be pack business," Pax explained.

"Shit," Donte swore. "Are you going to arrest me?"

Pax shook his head. "No. When Kade spoke to Connell, he said that if any arrests were going to be made, he wanted to plead guilty to Serge's too."

Donte frowned. "But I killed him."

"And we are going to pretend we didn't hear that," Coltrane smiled.

Donte's frown deepened as he took in everything that Coltrane said.

"Come on, let's go back to the compound; we can talk more about it then," I suggested.

Donte nodded, and I climbed back onto the bike behind him. Coltrane lifted his phone to his ear and spoke into it.

"We will get the Lancaster AJE unit out to cordon off the house. We'll see you guys later," Pax said.

I smiled and gave them a wave as Donte brought the bike to life and started back down the road toward Lalbert. My stomach curdled at the thought that Donte could be imprisoned for murder. I just hoped that somehow it could be all washed under the rug.

# Chapter Seven

S able
We weren't at the main Devil's Advocates compound before the head of the AJE authority arrived.

"Kade, this is the alphas of the Wild Claw Pack, Connell, Herrick, Fenris, Ward, and Sable. This is Kade Sinclair, the head of the AJE authority in Australia," Anghus introduced.

"It's nice to meet you all. I wish it was under better circumstances, however," Kade said before sitting down. "What can you all tell me?"

Connell sighed. "If there is going to be any arrests made, then I will be the one you arrest. I am solely responsible for the death of Kragen and Serge."

Kade nodded his head but didn't say anything. "Connell, you can't do that," Dad hissed.

Connell shook his head. "I won't have anyone else go down for this. It is on me."

Dad sighed. I could see that Connell was set.

"Are there going to be arrests made?" Lynx asked Kade.

The Nephilim breathed in deeply and scrubbed his hand over his face. "I'm in a bit of a tricky spot here. It would have been fine if these deaths had happened on pack lands. It would have been excused as pack business. Unfortunately, we have a slight problem because the deaths occurred in civilian areas."

"Serge was on Devil's Advocates land; would that make a difference?" Anghus asked.

Kade twisted his lips and nodded. "Possibly. I'm still waiting to hear back from Kyle Buchan, the supernatural prosecutor. He will be able to tell me more about what needs to happen. But at this stage, there is a likelihood that you will be arrested for at least Kragen's death. I can't give you any more than that. Bacchus explained that Kragen and Serge were Wild Claw Pack members, is that correct?"

Connell nodded his head. "Yes. Serge was my brother. He abducted my son when Donte was only a day old. I've been searching for them for twenty-seven years."

Kade nodded his head. "Were they ever officially cast out of the pack?"

Connell shook his head. "No. They left and went into hiding with Donte."

"That might be something we can use," he said as his phone rang. "Kyle, thanks for ringing me back. You heard? Yeah, I'm at the Devil's Advocates compound now. Alright. See you soon." Kade ended the call and looked up. "Kyle is going to come out here and meet us. Apparently, he isn't far away; he will be able to tell us more about what is likely to happen. But for now, I suggest you don't say anything else. And if you are going to take the fall for both deaths, do not implicate anyone.'"

Connell nodded but didn't say anything. It was only a few minutes before a knock on the door, and a man walked in. From his scent, I could tell he was a lion shifter.

"Alright, tell me what we've got. I've had a report from Lancaster; your boys are out there now; the body has been moved. And then there was a report of a death at the other Devil's compound," the man said.

"Thanks for coming, Kyle. These are the Wild Claw Pack, Connell, Herrick, Fenris, Ward, and Sable," Kade introduced. "The men killed were part of the Wild Claw Pack; they abducted Connell's son, Donte, twenty-seven years ago. The alphas have only just discovered where the abductors were."

Kyle nodded slowly as Kade told him the story. "Right. Well, we can scrub Serge's death off. That was done on what is considered pack lands. It wasn't Wild Claw land, but the Devil's Advocates compound is considered a pack land. However, for Kragen though, it was done in a civilian area. Who owns the house that Kragen was killed in?"

"No one. Well, neither Kragen nor Serge. From what I could find out, it had been abandoned when they took over, and they just stayed there," I said, remembering the information I'd sought.

Kyle looked over at me and nodded; he hummed in his throat. "Alright," he said as he twisted his lips before looking over at Anghus. "Is it alright that they stay on the compound for a few days?"

Anghus nodded his head. "Of course."

Kyle nodded and turned to Connell. "I've got to go and do some research; it's going to take me a couple of days. Can I trust that you won't take off, or do I need to take you into custody?"

Connell rolled his eyes. "I'm not going to go anywhere."

Kyle smiled and nodded. "I had a feeling you'd say that," he chuckled. "Alright, let me go and do some research. You've given me a bit of a dilemma. I think, though, that we can get you out of this easily. Unfortunately, you will probably be incarcerated for a little while, but it won't be long."

"Whatever needs to happen, I'll gladly take," Connell replied.

"Don't say anymore," Kyle answered, holding his hand up. "My only advice is don't say anything about the attack. And when the time comes to face the judges, pretend to be sad; I can see you're not, but pretend for their sake."

Kyle stood and said his goodbyes. Kade walked Kyle out of the house, and we sat silently staring at each other.

The front door swung open again, and a little boy came rushing in, holding the hand of the little girl.

"Iver," Anghus said. "You and Daisy are meant to be in classes."

Iver smirked at his father; looking at Anghus, I could see the gargoyle wasn't angry but more saying what he thought he was supposed to say.

"Daisy has a message," Iver said.

We all turned to the little girl, who began to sign what she was saying. She shook her head and sighed. Walking over to Connell, she reached out gently and laid her tiny hands on his cheeks.

Connell's eyes widened, and he gasped. "How?" he whispered.

The rest of us looked at each other with confusion. Tears welled in Connell's eyes and started to trek down his face.

"Iver, what is happening?" Anghus asked.

"Daisy had a message for Connell from Harley."

We all gasped in shock. There was no way that this little boy knew about Harley. Hell, I hadn't even known Harley. She'd died before I was born.

"I will, my love," Connell promised as he sniffed. Daisy slowly removed her hands from Connell's cheeks. He looked down into the little girl's face and sniffed again. "Thank you, little one."

Daisy grinned a toothy smile and turned to Iver. She signed something to him, and he grinned.

"You did good," he replied with a grin and signing.

"Is she deaf?" I asked.

Iver turned his attention to me and shook his head. "No. Daisy has Down Syndrome. She struggles to talk, so it's easier to use sign language. But she can speak and see spirits and help others see them when they need to share a message. This message was for Connell."

Connell nodded his head. "Yes. We need to move the pack."

My eyes widened. "To Lalbert?" I asked.

Connell looked over at me and nodded his head. "Yes. We need to be here for the war."

Anghus grinned, and Iver nodded his head before he turned to me. "And you are about to find out why you needed to be here."

I frowned and shook my head as the main house door opened and closed. I'd expected it to be Kade but instead saw Donte and his mate walk in. Standing as if being pulled by an unseen force, I walked towards them. Suddenly their scent hit, and my eyes rolled. I let out a groan.

Donte watched me with wide eyes while Savannah gasped. "A mate," she whispered.

I stopped, and my mouth dropped open in shock. "Oh my god," I gasped as I turned and looked back at my dad, who was grinning like a loon.

"My baby girl just found her mates. Holy shit," he laughed.

"With my son," Connell smiled.

Iver let out a giggle and walked towards Savannah. "Donte, Savannah? The creator wants you to know something."

We all turned to look at Iver. "What is it?" Donte asked.

"Once your mateship is complete with Sable, you will finally have that child you've always wanted."

Savannah gasped again, and tears pooled in her eyes. "Really?"

Iver nodded his head. "The timing was never right because you didn't have your final mate in place. But now that you are all together, you will be blessed with a little one."

Tears started to trek down Savannah's cheeks as she let out a sob. I moved on automatic and pulled her into my arms. Savannah wrapped her arms around my waist and buried her head into my neck. Holding her was strange; it was as if we'd always been together. I'd never felt this way towards someone. Donte's scent surrounded me as he pulled Savannah and me into his arms. I wrapped one arm around his back and held them both tight. They had been desperate to have a child, I could feel that desperation, and the whole time they'd been waiting for me. My head was spinning in shock. This was more than I could even comprehend.

Normally it was only mysticals that had poly mateship. But none of us were mysticals. I knew that Donte was a wolf. But I'd also been able to find out that Savannah was a spider shifter. And I was a wolf. There was something magical about this place. About these people and the thought had me so excited to be a part of it.

# Chapter Eight

D onte

I could hear everyone muttering around us, but I was having trouble focusing. There was so much going on. Sable's scent was overpowering me, then there was what Iver told us. We would finally have a baby. *We'd waited for a baby all this time and it was because we didn't have a third mate?* I just couldn't make sense of any of it.

Sable continued to hold Savannah as she quietly wept. I tried to work out in my mind if I was jealous. I had seen Kade leaving when we came in but hadn't had a chance to speak with him. It was like the whole world was slamming me at once. I didn't know which way to look.

"Focus on your mates right now," Connell said as he stood. "The rest will sort itself out soon."

I looked up at Connell. My father. Looking at him, I could see myself. We shared the same eyes.

Connell smiled and nodded his head. "We will talk later. Take your mate home. There is plenty of time for us."

I nodded my head silently. Home. Shit. I lived in the other compound with Savannah but only had my bike. I scratched at my chin as I tried to work out logistically how to get Sable back to our home as well.

Iver nudged me with his elbow as he came to stand beside me. I glanced down at the boy I'd taken a long time to get used to. It was weird to see a kid as intelligent and connected to the creator as Iver.

I leaned down so that he could whisper in my ear. "Sable rode her bike here too," he said.

My eyes widened as I realized that he had been able to pick up on my dilemma. I chuckled and kissed his cheek. "Thanks, kid." Iver grinned and nodded before returning to sit on the couch beside Daisy, watching us with her big blue eyes.

"Will we go home?" I asked quietly.

Sable and Savannah glanced up and nodded their heads. I had so much to think about. The ride home would give me a chance to get my head sorted.

"Don't hurry back," Anghus chuckled.

Herrick covered his ears and started singing a song that seemed familiar to me. I couldn't tell where I'd heard it before. I cocked my head to the side and frowned. Connell chuckled. "It is the song of our pack," he answered my inquisitive look.

"How would I know it?"

"Your Mama used to sing it when she was pregnant with you," he replied as tears rose. I could see the love that Connell had for my mother. I wanted to know more about her. I just hoped time would be on my side enough to get that chance.

Turning, I took Savannah's hand in mine and led her and Sable to where I'd parked my bike. Sable went to her bike and straddled the big chrome machine. I had to admit, it was fucking sexy to see her on there. Sable was gorgeous. I never thought I'd meet someone as beautiful as Savannah, but Sable was just as beautiful. She had almost white hair and grey eyes. She was Savannah's opposite. Sav had dark black hair and eyes that looked like molten chocolate.

"Are you sure you want this?" I asked Savannah before bringing the bike to life.

"With all of my heart, but I will not mate with Sable unless you want that," she said as she wrapped her arms around my middle.

"Then I guess we are about to get us a new mate," I said with a smile that made Savannah giggle.

With a roar, I brought my bike to life and slowly edged out of the compound, with Sable behind us. I wasn't sure if Gwen and Jantzen would still be at our place with Asher and March's kids, but I hoped they would have either been picked up or Gwen and Jantzen would have taken them back to their own home.

I had to take the time to speak with Asher and March and apologize for what must have been terrifying for the kids to witness. I hoped that they weren't too stressed about it. I knew that Gwen and Jantzen would have done their best to make them feel more comfortable. That was the kind of people they were.

I let out a long breath as the air whipped past my face, and the sun shone heavily down on my back. There is a saying that when it rains, it pours. I never even knew what that meant until this very moment. Here I was, learning that the people I thought were my fathers were my uncles, the man that is my father is now about to be possibly charged with murder. Not to mention taking on the responsibility for the death I caused. And on top of that, I am about to mate with another woman, an alpha woman, and Savannah would get pregnant.

Shit. What a fucking life. I couldn't even begin to think what Obsidian and the guys at work would think of all this. I was just going to be glad when I had a minute to breathe and process everything. Fuck there was so much to process.

# Chapter Nine

Savannah

I was stunned when I entered the compound's main house and caught Sable's scent. I don't think anyone could have quite shocked me more. But then, when Iver said I'd never had a baby because our family wasn't complete, I think I could have just about fainted.

Yet when Sable wrapped her arms around me, everything felt right. It felt like she was just meant to be part of our family. I was worried about what Donte would think about it. He did not take easily to change, but when he joined our hug, I knew that he was prepared to accept it.

By the time we reached the other compound, my body was overheating, and I felt like I was going into heat. I knew what this was. It was the same thing that had happened when I met Donte. It was the mating heat. The vibrations of the bike beneath me rumbled over my clit, and I felt my eyes unfocused as my mind narrowed in on the feeling.

When Donte killed the engine, I looked up at him, practically panting. Donte chuckled. "Well, I don't have to ask if you're ready for this."

I shook my head. "Donte, this is stronger than when I first met you."

Sable walked over to us and smiled. Her cheeks were blushed, and I could see she struggled as much as Donte and I. Donte's eyes widened, but judging by the evident bulge in his pants, I knew he was just as affected.

"That ride was hell," Sable groaned with a husky voice.

Donte chuckled again. "I think Sav would agree. Come on let's get inside."

I climbed from the bike, took Donte's hand in one and Sable's in the other, and walked towards our front door. As soon as we were inside and the door was locked, we all stood staring at each other. Suddenly I realized I had no idea what to do. I'd never been with another woman. I mean, I wasn't naïve. I'd watched porn. But I didn't know what to do.

"Can I kiss you?" Sable asked, looking down at me.

I looked up into her grey eyes, biting down on my bottom lip; I nodded my head. Sable smiled as she stepped toward me and took my cheeks in her hands. Slowly she lowered her mouth to mine. It felt strange. First, her lips were softer; there was no stubble from a beard. But the minute her tongue swept into my mouth, I groaned. All my thoughts floated away, and I could only focus on making her mine.

I stepped closer, pulling Sable by the hips against my body. Sable moaned against my lips as she continued to kiss me with such passion, I thought I could literally float away. Donte growled in the background. He had always had a thing for watching lesbian scenes. I giggled as I broke the kiss and looked over my shoulder at Donte.

He had stripped out his shirt and unzipped his jeans that rode low on his hips. "Do you like what you see?" I asked breathlessly.

"You've no idea how fucking sexy that is," he growled, causing Sable and I to giggle.

"I think, though, that Savannah might need your guidance," Sable said.

Donte moaned, and I saw the lust in his eyes. This was precisely what he wanted.

"Sav, take Sable's shirt off," Donte instructed. His voice was deep and full of growl. I'd never heard it like that before, and to say it did things to me would be an understatement.

I turned my attention back to Sable and reached for the hem of her black t-shirt. I slowly slipped it over her head and allowed it to drop to the floor. Sable smiled down at me and reached for my hips. She turned my body, so my back was facing hers, and I looked at Donte. He had hold of his bulge through his jeans and licked over his bottom lip.

Sable reached for the hem of the pink shirt I'd been wearing and lifted it slowly from my body. She moaned as she realized I wasn't wearing a bra beneath. Gently with featherlight touches, Sable stroked her fingers across my stomach and sides. Skimming the underside of my breasts, I watched Donte's eyes dilate. His wolf was pushing to the front, and I knew it wouldn't be long before he couldn't hold himself back.

Moaning as Sable flicked her fingertips over my nipples, I kept my eyes on Donte. I knew that this wasn't just the heat. I was horny, hornier than I'd ever been. Sable rolled my pebbled nipples in her fingers. The feeling shot like an electric pulse straight to my clit. I pressed my thighs together and moved my hips, feeling the crotch of my jeans cause friction where I needed it most.

"Both of you, take your clothes off. Then, Sable, I want you to sit on the couch with Sav on your lap and spread your legs wide. I want to taste you both," Donte growled.

My eyes rolled just at his words. Sable moaned in my ear and reached for my jeans. Once we were both naked, she did precisely as Donte directed. Sitting on her lap, she spread my thighs coated in my juices. I didn't think I'd ever been quite so wet before.

I didn't know when it happened, but when I looked at Donte, he was suddenly naked. He crawled across the carpet to where Sable and I sat, ready for him. Sable stroked my breasts as she kissed my neck and shoulders. That alone had my eyes rolling, but the minute Donte's tongue slid over my clit, down over my hole, I was practically screaming with need.

Donte continued to lap at us both. My toes were curled, and Sable's breaths in my ear as she moaned brought my pleasure higher. Finally, Donte curled his tongue around my clit and sucked it from its hood into his mouth. Pressing his lips firmly around my button, I cried out as gushes of juices slipped from me, coating Donte's chin.

"Fuck, yes," Sable moaned.

"Press on her clit," Donte demanded.

No sooner had he moved his mouth from my pussy, than Sable had her fingers keeping firm pressure on my clit. Her moans bounced around the room as Donte brought her closer and closer to the edge.

"I need to fuck you," Donte said. I didn't know how, but I knew he wasn't talking to me.

Suddenly Donte's hands were on my waist, and he was lifting me in the air and turning me in Sable's lap. Sable threaded her hands through my hair and pulled me down, sweeping her tongue into my mouth to tangle with mine.

I groaned and rocked my pussy back and forth against her as I felt Donte step in behind me. Sable gasped as Donte filled her and started to fuck into her as a man possessed.

He bit into my neck, licking to salve the sting. Sable's hands roamed over my body as Donte grunted with every thrust.

As I looked into Sable's eyes, I watched the moment I knew she would mate with me. Her eyes flashed the same gold that Donte's did when his wolf was close to the surface. Her incisors grew, and she leaned forward.

"Now," Donte growled as he leaned over my shoulder and bit into Sable.

I screamed as my orgasm washed over me, just as Donte pulled out of Sable and pushed his cock into my pussy, and Sable's teeth pierced my skin. My incisors lengthened, and I leaned forward, biting into Sable's chest as she returned Donte's bite.

Donte roared as his knot locked hard inside me and pulsed as he filled me with his seed. This was it. I could feel it. I had conceived. Slowly my breathing returned to normal, and I sighed. I opened my eyes and looked up at Sable and Donte, who was watching me.

"You are so fucking beautiful," Sable said, causing me to giggle.

I leaned forward and kissed her gently on the lips.

"I am never going to get sick of seeing that," Donte growled from behind me, causing Sable and I to laugh.

"I'm pregnant," I whispered, glancing over my shoulder. Donte blinked, and I could see the concern on his face. He wanted to believe me but didn't want to get his hopes up. "You'll see."

Donte kissed my shoulder. "I hope so, baby. I really hope so."

"Me too," Sable said. "That boy Iver. He is powerful?"

I nodded my head. "Everyone that is part of the Devil's Advocates is powerful."

Sable nodded. "I think the Wild Claw Pack will be moving here too."

"Yeah?" Donte said.

Sable nodded her head. "Yeah. Before you came back, the little girl Daisy allowed Harley, your Mama, to come through to Donte. She gave him a message about moving here."

"Holy shit," Donte said with a shake of his head.

"There is a lot we need to learn and understand," I said.

"You got that right, baby," Donte replied with a chuckle. "Shit, yesterday I was just a mechanic doing my thing. And today, I've got two mates, possibly a child on the way and a real biological father. And two dead cunts that had lied to me for years."

# Chapter Ten

# D
onte

I think I could die a happy man. Watching Sable and Savannah together was my most fantastic fantasy come to life. I'd never seen anything so sexy. We spent the rest of the day in bed, alternating between all of us and one on one. Even Savannah said she was getting off on watching Sable and me together. I couldn't believe how easily we had all just come together. It was weird; Mother fate had outdone herself.

When we dragged ourselves out of bed the following day, my mind was full of everything I had to do. First, I needed to go and speak to Obsidian. I was going to need to take some time off. I wanted to sort out everything with Connell. Then I had to talk to Anghus about getting us a bigger house. The apartment we currently were in was a one bedroom. It had suited us when it was just Savannah and me, but now that we had Sable and possibly a child on the way, we needed something larger.

I had some savings that we had put away, so I knew we would be able to purchase a bigger house on the Devil's Advocates compound. We needed to really talk about where we wanted to go to. There was just so much to do.

I dragged myself out of bed and turned to see Sable and Savannah migrate into the center of the bed toward each other. It was amazing at the pull they seemed to have. I loved it. Moving into the shower, I glanced at the mating mark Sable left on my chest, opposite Savannah's. I smiled as I fingered the spot. I couldn't believe that this was real.

Chuckling to myself, I got washed and dried before dressing in a fresh pair of jeans and a t-shirt. Savannah and Sable were still asleep. I crept to the bed and placed a small kiss on either of their cheeks. Savannah moaned in her sleep while Sable let out a sigh and tightened her arms around Savannah's waist. I smiled. My girls. Damn, I was a fucking lucky man.

By the time I reached Obsidian Mechanics, my head was a little clearer, and I had a list going with everything I needed to do. I pulled up outside and strode into the office, where Alena was printing off the day's to-do list. She glanced up and gave me a wicked grin.

"Well, if it isn't the man of the hour," she said with a laugh.

I chuckled and rapped my knuckles on the desk in front of her. "Is Obsidian in?"

"Sure is; I think he is waiting for you with excitement," Alena said with another laugh.

I barked out a laugh and nodded my head. So, it seems that my news has traveled fast. I wondered who I might have to thank for that one. Anghus probably, he was the biggest gossip going. I walked over to Obsidian's office and knocked lightly on the door. When I heard him call out, I swung the door open with a smile.

"Donte. The man with the new mate," Obsidian chuckled.

"Hey, man. I'm sorry for running out yesterday."

Obsidian shook his head. "Don't stress about it. Anghus explained everything."

I was right. It was Anghus who had told.

"I don't like to leave you short, but I was hoping I could grab a couple of days off; I want to sort out some things with Connell. Especially if he is going to be sent away for Kragen's death."

Obsidian nodded his head and waved his hand. "Don't stress; take all the time you need."

"Thanks, man. It should only be a couple of days."

Obsidian nodded and smiled. "How are you coping with everything?"

I sighed and sat in the seat opposite my boss and a man I honestly thought of as a friend.

"To be honest, I think I'm still in shock. Everything is so overwhelming. Not just with Sable. But with finding out about my dad. The men I thought were my fathers were just assholes that kidnapped me.

I can't get past it. And part of me thinks I should be sad that they are dead. I feel like an asshole because I'm happy."

"I don't think you should feel like an asshole. I think I'd feel exactly the same way. Just take your time. Go slow. One day at a time, and know I'm always here if you need someone to talk to."

"Thanks, Sid. I really appreciate it. I just need to go and speak to Connell. I think I need to know everything, you know. It's just weird."

"Is it worth taking some time to talk to Alexandria?" Obsidian asked.

I shrugged my shoulders. It was a good suggestion, and maybe I would make some time to speak to the Devil's Advocates psychologist. If for nothing else, just to have someone help me sort out my thoughts and reassure me that what I was feeling wasn't bad.

"Maybe. Anyway, I better go. I don't know how long it will be before Kade comes and arrests Connell."

Obsidian smiled and stood. He reached out his arms and pulled me into a tight hug. "Anything you need, you come and speak to me. We are your family too."

"Thank you. I appreciate you."

Obsidian patted me on the back, and I turned, leaving the office and heading out towards my bike. I meant it. I appreciated everything Obsidian and the Rigby family had done for Savannah and me. I couldn't express how much their love and support meant to me.

# Chapter Eleven

S able

It felt strange to have someone on the back of my bike as I rode back towards the main compound. Savannah had taken me all over the secondary Devil's Advocates compound where she lived. The place was amazing. I thought our pack lands were unique, but they had nothing on the Devil's Advocates compounds. The site was a complete, fully functioning little city.

They had gardens that grew vegetables and fruits, an orchard, chickens, cows, and sheep. They had everything they needed. Savannah introduced me to many of the omegas that the Devil's Advocates had rescued over the years and explained about the schools they ran. Everything she showed me blew my mind.

We pulled up to the main house, and I noticed that Donte's bike was already parked out the front. Children played in front of a large building.

"That's the school building for this compound. Most of the kids go there, but some of the omegas preferred staying at the secondary compound, so Anghus set up a school building there too," Savannah explained.

I shook my head. "This place is absolutely amazing. I can't get over how much there is here."

Savannah smiled and nodded her head. "Anghus wanted to give the omegas rescued from the breeding facilities a new life. He wanted to show them what living in freedom was really like. He'd been rescued from Morpheus, so he wanted to save others."

I nodded. I loved it. Everyone I'd met seemed so happy. The omegas I was introduced to all seemed grateful to have the opportunity to live in freedom. I was highly impressed by it and couldn't wait to get more involved. Of course, the Wild Claw Pack moving to Lalbert excited me too. That had been my only worry. I hated the idea of being too far away from Dad and Lobo. We were a close family, even closer since Mama died. To have them nearby would be perfect.

"Come on, let's get inside. I can feel your dad's worry from here," Savannah laughed.

I followed her up the stairs towards the main house. My attention zeroed in on Donte the minute we rounded the corner. I'd really got lucky. My mates were fucking gorgeous. A series of wolf whistles sounded as we walked into the living room. I laughed, and when I glanced at Savannah, her cheeks blushed, but she looked happy.

"Sav," a young guy said with a smile. He stood from the couch with a baby in his arms as he came toward her and pulled Savannah into a tight hug.

"March, this is my other mate, Sable. This is my brother March."

Savannah had told me that she was one of twenty children. I was in shock when I heard it. Twenty. I couldn't even imagine having that many.

"It's really nice to meet you, March."

March smiled and held his arms open for a hug. I stepped into his arms and wrapped him up in a bear hug.

"We need to discuss some things now that Sable is here," Dad said.

I nodded my head and stepped over to sit beside Donte. Savannah sat in his lap, and we waited to find out what would happen.

"Kade came back yesterday. They are going to lay charges on Connell today; they wanted to wait until Donte was back, well, they didn't, but Bacchus here has some sway, it seems," Dad explained.

"Are you being charged with just Kragen or both deaths?" I asked Connell.

"Just Kragen. Apparently, they were able to consider the Devil's Advocates compound as pack land. But Kragen, they couldn't get around it."

I nodded my head. "So, what happens?"

"Kyle, the prosecutor believes that if I plead guilty, I will be given a maximum term of five years."

I hissed. Five years. It wasn't a long time, but it was. It would leave the Wild Claw Pack without its ruling alpha. Ward would step in as he was the secondary alpha, but it didn't change the fact that we would be without Connell, and he would be in prison. We wouldn't have anyone there to protect him.

"And there isn't any way we can get him out of it?" I asked, looking over at Bacchus.

Bacchus shook his head. "No. I'm sorry. The shifter units and Kade have tried our hardest to find a solution. Asher, my brother," he said, pointing over at an older man holding March's baby. "He has been in contact with his lawyer, but apparently, there is no way around it. Although supernatural law works differently from human law, Connell still has to face punishment for Kragen's death."

"And five years is the least they will give him?" Donte questioned.

Bacchus nodded his head. "Hopefully. Of course, his sentence ultimately is up to a judge. But Kyle can put forth his recommendation that Connell only receives a five-year sentence."

"Where will he be sent to?" I questioned.

"There is a supernatural prison in Melbourne. I know that Kade tried to find out if it would be possible for Connell to serve his sentence out here in Lalbert at the AJE authority precinct, but Kyle said they would never go for it."

I chewed on my bottom lip as I pondered everything. I didn't like the idea of sending Connell into prison without protection. Dad looked over at me and seemed to be able to read my mind.

"What do we know about the prison?" Connell asked.

"Ashtomb correctional facility. That's where you would be sent to; it is maximum security. All inmates are there for murder," Bacchus explained.

"Shit," Donte growled. "I don't like this at all. Do we have members that are staff there?"

Suddenly the front door swung open, and I saw Kade walking in when I looked up. "Ah, good you're all here. I need to talk more about what is going to happen."

"We were just talking about the prison. Are there people we can trust to look out for Connell?" Donte asked.

Kade smirked and sat down on the floor. "I was just coming to talk to you about it," he said with a chuckle. "As you know, we are about to head into a war situation. Ettore, my brother and Nephilim, wants to enslave and kill the supernatural population and humans. He wants to bring demons earthside and rule the earth. He has teamed up with several not very nice supernaturals. Two of which have recently escaped prison. Blaise Knight and Vex Blakely. We know that Nystrom is dead, thanks to Oakland. And Granger Redburn is still currently incarcerated. Ettore hasn't been able to get him out yet. But we know that Ettore has made contact with Granger and has offered him something to bring him to his side. So, if you are willing, Connell, maybe we can use this situation to our advantage?"

"What are you suggesting?" Connell asked.

"While incarcerated, you try to form a friendship with Granger. Find out what he knows about Ettore's plans and feed them back to us, allowing us to be in front of him a bit more."

Connell hummed and nodded his head. He looked around the room.

"I'll do it."

# Chapter Twelve

**D**onte

I hated this. I couldn't explain it. But I felt a bond so strong with Connell and all of the Wild Claw Pack. I'd pulled Connell into my arms and held him tight before Kade took him away. As much as I liked Kade's plan of using Connell as a plant within Ashtomb prison, I was nervous. This meant that Connell would be alone, without any of his pack. And it wasn't like we could just go in and get him out if it all went wrong.

I didn't know what my mother said to Connell when she appeared to him with Daisy, but he was determined to do this. He promised to share everything with me one day, but it wasn't the right time at that moment. Kade told us that Connell was set to appear before the panel of supernatural judges early next week. Kyle, the prosecutor, had accepted the plea deal he'd come up with and was putting it forward. Kyle suggested that we were hoping for a maximum of five years, but ultimately it would be up to the judges.

All I could be thankful for was that we were supernatural, and the laws worked differently for us. They would have locked Connell up and thrown away the key if we were human. But then again, maybe the police would have done something about my abduction if we were human. As it was, Connell and Harley never used the AJE authority when I was abducted. It was pack business; they knew who took me and were determined to find them. However, I couldn't help but wonder if they had gone to the AJE authority if I'd been found sooner. Maybe I wouldn't have gone through the hell I did if they had. But it was in the past, and there was nothing I could do about it now.

We were all sitting in the garden, soaking in the sun at the main compound. "Donte, will you tell us about what happened to you?" Ward asked, glancing over at me.

They had just finished giving me the rundown of the Wild Claw Pack. My father, Connell was the top alpha; he was the first alpha born. Then Ward, Fenris, and Herrick were the other alphas. Apparently, with every generation, there were four male alphas born. Out of the four current alphas, I was the firstborn, then Herrick had Lobo, Sable's brother. Fenris and Ward were yet to be mated.

I sighed and scrubbed my hands over my face. "It was shit. There was a lot of pain. Serge and Kragen hated me, which is why I don't understand why they took me. I mean, if they wanted a child of their own, they suddenly had one, you'd think they would have loved me and cherished me," I said with a shake of my head.

Sable laced her fingers with mine and gave my hand a squeeze. Savannah had a shift at Ellie's café.

"They beat me practically every day. Serge stubs his toe, I get beaten, Kragen's football team loses, so I get beaten. It was like any little thing that could piss them off; they would beat me as if it were my fault. But what was worse, was when they figured out, they could make money off me."

Ward and Fenris shared a look, and I could see the fury in Herrick's eyes when he looked at me. "What did they do?"

I breathed in deeply. This was a part of my life that I rarely spoke about. Savannah knew but not all of it. I kept a lot of it inside. I knew it wasn't healthy; it had made me a furious young man. But I always credited Savannah as my savior. She was the one that kept me safe.

"When I was seven years old, Kragen met some pedophile. I don't know where he met him; I don't even know who he was. But somehow, this pedo struck up a deal with Kragen and Serge. At first, Serge wasn't onboard," I said with a snort. "Like pedophilia was beneath him. Anyway, Kragen managed to talk Serge into it, and a week later, I was sold to be a waiter for this pedo and his friends. At first, I had to walk around in girls' underwear and serve them food on plates. Most of them didn't touch me, and I could live with it. I didn't like it, I was humiliated beyond belief, but it was better than what was to come."

I breathed in deeply again as I thought about where it ended up going. Tears burned at my eyes, and I bit into my bottom lip, wobbling with the weight of my grief.

"It was my tenth birthday when it changed. I don't know if it was because Kragen and Serge didn't give the pedo's permission or if it was that the pedophile held back before that time. I don't know. But on my tenth birthday, the pedo came to pick me up, and I thought we were just doing the same thing as usual. But this time, he told me to lie on the table in the dining room. I did what I was told. But tried to fight when he started to tie me down. I was able to shift by then, so I tried shifting, but that was when I realized I'd been strapped down by silver and couldn't shift."

The tears I'd been holding back started to trek down my cheeks as the memory of what happened after that. The pain, I had never felt anything like it. I vomited, and they still didn't stop. It didn't matter how much I begged or cried. It was like they got off on my pain.

"They raped you, didn't they?" Herrick growled.

Sable gasped and pulled me into her chest. She held me tight and stroked down over my back, whispering gently into my ear. I bit into my bottom lip and nodded my head.

"How many?" Ward asked.

"I don't remember. But at least seven," I mumbled into Sable's neck.

"Do you know any of their names?" Herrick asked.

I lifted my head and sighed. "No. I never knew their names. I was never told."

"Fuck I wish we knew about this before we killed that cunt. I would've hunted each of them down," Herrick growled.

Their anger was strange. I'd never had anyone get angry for my sake. I'd never had anyone other than Savannah who cared about me enough to get mad for my sake. *Was this what it was like to actually have a family?*

# Chapter Thirteen

S avannah

"Well, if it isn't the lady of the hour," Mitchell laughed as I walked into Ellie's staff room. I'd been working at the café since we first came to Lalbert. It was a great vegan place, so I didn't have to touch meat. The only beef I liked was Donte and, well, now Sable. I blushed as memories of what had happened flooded my mind. *Who knew adding a third could turn our love-making into something so fucking hot?*

I giggled and waved my hand at Mitchell. He was a perpetual romantic. He loved the idea of mates. But had yet to find his own. I always hoped that one day that special someone would walk in off the street and be Mitchell's. He was one of the sweetest guys I knew. He treated everyone with so much love and didn't judge a soul. Yet it felt like Mother fate just kept passing him by.

The entire time I knew him, I hadn't seen him dating anyone. Even when I pointed out cute boys and girls to him, he would wave me off and tell me when it was time, it would be time. I couldn't help it, though; I wanted everyone to experience the same happiness that I had. And now that happiness was doubled.

"So, tell me about this new mystery mate?" he asked as I put my apron on and tied it around my waist.

I sighed. "Her name is Sable. She is a wolf shifter. It was all so strange how it happened. But it felt like it was meant to be. I mean, it was. But yeah, just weird."

"Is she hot?"

I grinned and nodded my head. "You've no idea. She is tall like Donte, with almost white hair, grey eyes, and a body to die for. Sexy as sin." I giggled as I picked up the tablet I used to wait tables and walked into the café.

We weren't overly busy, which gave me a chance to do all the little jobs I had to do, like fill the salt and pepper shakers and top up the serviettes. I glanced around the dining room and noticed a couple of the regulars that came in every morning for coffee before they headed off to their business.

"Good morning, Charlotte," I said with a smile to the young lady that came in every morning. She had the same thing, a soy hot chocolate, and a chocolate muffin. She was one of the women I had tried to set Mitchell up with. However, he said he just wasn't interested.

"Hey, Savannah. I missed you yesterday. Mitchell said that you have met your mate," Charlotte said with a grin.

I smiled and nodded my head. "Well, a second mate. I was already mated to Donte. But Sable came into our lives, purely by chance."

"That is so romantic. So, will children be following soon?"

I breathed in deeply and smiled. "I sure hope so," I said as I skimmed my hand down over my stomach.

I got the feeling that I was pregnant. I felt it the moment that Donte's knot had locked in me when we all mated. But it would be a few more days until I could get confirmation. I could have asked Iver, but I'd find out through a pregnancy test. I always felt guilty when the omegas asked Iver about their babies. I kind of felt like they often used him as a bit of a circus freak. I didn't want to do that. His powers were spectacular; I didn't want to belittle them by using him as a general fortune teller.

"I can't wait to finally be able to meet my mate," Charlotte said with a sigh.

"I'm sure they will come one day," I replied.

Charlotte sighed again and shrugged her shoulders. "Sometimes, I wonder if Mother fate has forgotten me."

"I used to wonder the same thing about children. I wondered if I'd done something wrong in my life and wouldn't be blessed with them. But then she sent Sable at the right time."

Charlotte smiled and nodded her head as she popped the last of her muffin in her mouth and chewed. "I guess that's it; I've just got to wait for the right time."

I smiled down at Charlotte. Reaching out, I gave her shoulder a squeeze. I believed that there was someone out there for everyone. None of us was meant to be alone. Maybe I was the one that was the perpetual romantic. But I'd always thought that. I looked at my Mama and Papa's mateship; they had an excellent relationship. As did the Rigby family and those mated at the Devil's Advocates. We were all meant to have someone; it was just a matter of being in the right place at the right time to find them. Or, in my case, wait for them to rock up and kill who I thought was my father-in-law.

# Chapter Fourteen

S able
Hearing Donte's story had made me so fucking angry. I wanted to hunt down every bastard that hurt my mate and destroy them. But one of the Wild Claw Pack was already in prison; I didn't need to be shoved in beside Connell. Although, at least he would be protected.

It was a week before Connell went before the judges. I'd been nervous and knew that the others were worried too. However, it had gone a lot more smoothly than we had expected.

"We have looked over the plea deal that the prosecutor has supplied us as well as the evidence we were given by your solicitor and have heard your guilty plea. Therefore, we are satisfied that you won't re-offend, and this was a one-off issue. Had it happened on pack lands, as you are aware, you wouldn't be in this position. Unfortunately for you, that didn't happen. We can't overlook that you took a man's life in a civilian area, regardless of what kind of monster that man was. Our supernatural laws say clearly that this is something that won't happen in civilian areas. In saying all of that, however, we recognize that this was a pack issue. Kragen was still considered part of the Wild Claw Pack and therefore came under the law of that pack. This is why we will be sentencing you to two years imprisonment at the Ashtomb Correctional Facility," the judge said before banging his hammer on the gavel in front of him.

There was a collective sigh of relief as we heard the sentence. Connell was getting less than what we had been preparing for. We'd expected a five-year sentence, but the judges decided on two instead. That was fantastic. It would be enough time for Connell to have a chance to befriend Granger Redburn and hopefully get the information that the AJE authority needed. Still, it wasn't too long.

I watched as two guards came and walked Connell out of the room through a side door. Kubo, his solicitor that Asher Rigby had organized, spoke quietly to Connell before he left. Connell smiled and nodded his head. He looked over at us and gave a solid nod.

"Let's go out to the hall before we talk," Kubo said as he walked toward us.

As a pack, we left the courtroom and mingled in the hallway. Donte, Anghus, and Israel had joined us at the courthouse to hear the sentence.

"Kade is going to be meeting Connell at the prison. I can't say for sure what is going on behind the scenes, but I know that Kade is setting many things up for Connell to be both safe and to help in the war," Kubo said.

"Thank you for your help," Fenris said as he stuck his hand out for Kubo.

Kubo nodded and shook Fenris's hand before shaking the rest of ours. Kyle stepped toward us with a smile on his face.

"That went better than we were expecting," he said.

I smiled and nodded my head. "He will be safe?" I asked.

Kyle smiled and nodded. "Yep. I can't talk too much about it here. But Connell is safe. He will be kept safe."

I breathed out and smiled. "Thank the gods."

Kyle smiled and said his goodbyes.

"I guess we should get back to the pack and organize this move then," Dad said.

Ward nodded his head. "Yeah. Shit, we've got a lot to do."

Fenris scrubbed his hands up over his face and sighed. "Tell me about it. I can't even begin to think about the logistics. You know that bloody Connell has caused us a bit of a nightmare."

Dad laughed and nodded his head. "Yeah, while he is luxuriating in prison, we have all the hard work."

Ward snorted and slapped Dad on the back. "Well, Lobo has been doing an excellent job. Apparently, he was able to make a start on gathering up what we will need to purchase land."

"I was just about to ask, what you had planned to do about pack lands," Donte said.

Ward smiled. "We've been having a look over some properties while you've been busy with your mates," he said with a wiggle of his brows, making me laugh and my father gag. Ward chuckled. "We've found a couple we like that will be big enough for the pack."

"Where?" I asked.

"Actually, right next to the secondary compound. It shares a border. The other is further out towards Lancaster. But the one we hope to get is near the compound," Ward explained.

"That would be excellent. You know we were happy to let you all live in the compound," Anghus said.

Ward waved his hand. "I know. But Connell wanted a place that was ours. Plus, you have to keep the room open for more omegas. After spending the last week getting to know about Ettore, I know that there are going to be a lot of people that are going to be misplaced once the facilities he is running shut down."

Anghus sighed and nodded his head. "Yeah, that's true. With the numbers that we are currently looking at, we are even considering having to get more land."

My eyes widened. I knew that Ettore still owned many facilities, but the compounds that the Devil's Advocates owned were huge. It was hard to believe that they could ever be too full.

"Have you decided yet where you want to build a family home?" Anghus asked, turning his attention to Donte.

Donte nodded his head. We had talked a lot over the last week about a property. We still didn't know if Savannah was pregnant. Life had been a bit hectic, and we hadn't had a chance to slow down long enough to do a pregnancy test. Yet I knew that now the sentencing was done, we would have the opportunity to focus on our lives a little more.

"Yeah, we wanted to stay at the secondary compound. We've made good friends there and enjoy being there."

Anghus smiled. "I know that Mama and Papa will be glad you are all staying out there. They love you all."

I smiled. I felt the same about Gwen and Jantzen. Gwen had come from a breeding facility, and Jantzen was Ettore's stepson. It was hard to believe they had come from such a hard life. But they were such loving and caring people.

"We will go over the plans with you. There are a couple of houses ready to move into, but if you'd rather build, you can do that too," Anghus said.

Donte smiled but shook his head. "Na man, I was going to buy an already built house off you."

Anghus frowned and shook his head. "What is it with these people who keep wanting to give us money for their houses?"

Israel chuckled. "They don't want to use your generosity, man; just accept it and put the money back into the compound. You know you will anyway. And there is plenty that is going to need the houses that don't have the money."

"Yeah, just take the money," Donte said.

Anghus chuckled and sighed. "Alright. Well, when we get back, tell me which house you want, and we will organize some guys to come and help you move in."

"Thanks, man. Everything you've done for my family means a lot. Not just me and Savannah, but for the Wild Claw Pack too."

Anghus winked and reached out a big arm, pulling Donte into his chest. He kissed Donte on the head. "You know that you are family to me. That means the Wild Claw Pack is family too."

I breathed in deeply. I loved that. We were family.

# Chapter Fifteen

S avannah
I had the pregnancy test sitting on the bathroom cabinet at home. I was waiting for Donte and Sable to get home before I took it, but my patience was thin. I wanted to know if I was pregnant. I'd asked Sable last night if there was a chance she was pregnant. Even though Sable was an alpha she still was a woman and had all the same reproductive organs as any other woman. Meaning that she could still be pregnant. It wasn't like we used contraception.

It would be fun to have a baby with my mate simultaneously. But then again, two babies running around at the same age could get tiring. Not that I was expected to do it all on my own. I knew that Donte would be a fantastic father, and from what I'd recently learned about Sable, she would be a great mother.

Finally, the front door swung open, and Donte came in with Sable. They both smiled happily at me as they went into the living room.

"Did the court case go alright?" I asked. Although Kyle had said he was putting forward a five-year sentence, it was ultimately up to the judges to decide. I'd been worried about Connell.

Donte nodded his head. "Yep, better than we expected. The judges gave him two years."

My eyes widened as a smile crept across my lips. "That's fantastic news. So, um, I bought a pregnancy test."

Donte's smile was beaming. "Have you done it yet?"

I shook my head and bit into my bottom lip. "I wanted to wait until you were both home so we can celebrate together if it's positive."

"Well, what are you waiting for, woman? Get on in there and do it," Donte said with a laugh as he grabbed my shoulders, turned me around, and popped me on the backside.

I giggled as I entered the bathroom and opened the box holding the pregnancy test. A knock sounded on the bathroom door, and Sable poked her head around. "Do you mind if I come in?"

I shook my head. "Of course not, but I haven't done a wee yet."

Sable laughed and waved her hand. "I can handle seeing that."

"I bought an extra test, in case you wanted to try too," I explained as I held up the second box.

Sable chewed on her lip as she looked at the box. I couldn't tell what was going through her mind, but she seemed nervous. I didn't know if that was about the possibility that I wouldn't be pregnant or the possibility that she would be. Pulling the test out of the box, I pulled down my pants and sat on the toilet. I started to urinate before sticking the test between my legs and ensuring I'd coated the test strip.

Once I was done and had flushed the toilet, I washed my hands and stared down at the test. Sable was still staring off in the distance, and I could tell she was wrestling with something in her mind.

"Penny, for your thoughts?" I asked.

Sable blinked at looked at me. She glanced down at the test, and her eyes widened as if she hadn't realized that I'd already taken the test and was just waiting.

"I want to try the test, but I'm nervous," Sable admitted. Her cheeks blushed.

"What are you nervous about?"

Sable breathed in deeply before slowly letting it out. "I don't know, really. I'd love to have a baby grow in my belly. But I lost my mum when I was thirteen years old. I don't really know how to be a mum."

I nodded my head and reached out my hand to take hers. Pulling Sable towards me, I wrapped my arms around her waist and held her against my chest.

"I think you would be a wonderful mother. You know about Donte's upbringing and look how he is with the kids here at the compound. He will make a fantastic Dad despite what Kragen and Serge did to him."

Sable nodded her head. It was true. All of the kids adored Donte. It didn't matter how grumpy he looked; the kids still flocked to him. They knew that he was a good man. I liked to believe that kids had an extraordinary intuition about that.

"Alright, I'll try," Sable said with a slight giggle before she ripped open the box and shoved her pants down, and sat on the toilet before urinating onto the stick.

"I'll turn mine over so we can check it with yours," I said as I flipped the test while Sable washed her hands.

"Should we call Donte in?" Sable asked. "I don't feel like he should be left out."

I smiled and opened the bathroom door. Donte was already standing on the other side, looking expectantly. I giggled and waved our mate into the room.

"Sable took a test too; we are going to wait for hers to be ready and then read them both out," I explained as Donte crowded into the tiny bathroom of our apartment.

"I'm looking forward to moving to one of the bigger houses," Donte said as he looked around at how tightly squeezed in we were.

"Have you spoken to Anghus about it yet?" I asked.

Donte nodded his head. "Yep. We are going to meet up tomorrow to pick out the house. I wanted to do it with you, so you were included."

I smiled and leaned forward, standing on my toes; I pressed my lips to Donte's. "Thank you. I love you," I murmured.

Donte smiled and kissed me back. "I love you too."

I turned around and looked down briefly at Sable's test. "Alright, ready?" Sable nodded and lifted her stick while I picked mine up. "In three. One. Two. Three."

We turned the tests around simultaneously, and I gasped. There were two pink lines on my test. I was pregnant. Oh, my stars. I was going to have a baby.

"Well, what do they say?" Donte asked. He was practically bouncing on his toes with anticipation.

I looked up at him and smiled. "I'm pregnant," I replied before looking to Sable, who looked a mixture of shock, confused, happy and scared.

"I'm pregnant too," she whispered.

Donte lifted his head and let out a long howl. "I'm going to be a Papa. And I'm going to have two babies. You girls have made me the happiest man on earth."

I giggled and pulled both Sable and Donte into my arms. We were a family, and it was going to be growing. I couldn't believe how long I'd wanted a baby, and now finally, it was here. I was going to be a Mama. Not just to one baby. But two.

# Chapter Sixteen

Sable

I was still in shock about being pregnant, three months had passed, and the Wild Claw Pack was getting ready for the move any day now. There was a huge amount of excitement for our babies. Not only because of me; but because these children would be the heir holders of the Wild Claw Pack. I was excited; there was no question about it. Even though it felt like my whole world was moving too fast. One minute we were looking for Connell's lost son, and the next, I was mated; Connell was in prison, the Wild Claw Pack were moving from Trentham to Lalbert, I was pregnant, and so was my mate. No wonder I was exhausted.

"Are you excited about the ultrasound?" Savannah asked as we lay in bed before getting up and going to our doctor's appointments.

"I am. I think my head is finally catching up with everything that has happened in the last three months."

Savannah laughed and nodded. "The world has been moving very fast for you. I'm glad, though, that you are here with us."

I smiled down at my mate and kissed the top of her head. "Me too."

Savannah's cheeks blushed when she looked up at me. "I love you, Sable."

My eyes widened. I had been in love with Savannah and Donte the minute I mated with them. But I was yet to hear it from them and yet to say it myself.

"I love you too," I replied. I leaned forward and pressed my lips to Savannah's. With a groan, she swept her tongue against mine. Pulling her tighter against my body, I moved my leg between hers.

Instantly Savannah began to grind against my thigh. Stroking my hands up and down all over her body. I cupped her breasts and flicked my thumb over her nipples, delighting in the gasps that fell from her lips.

"Fuck, I love seeing that," Donte groaned from the door. Savannah and I broke our kiss to look at our other mate, who leaned against the door jam. "Don't stop. I want to watch."

He unzipped his jeans and slid them down his hips enough to release his cock, which was hard and angry looking. Spitting into his hand, he started to stroke his shaft. I moved Savannah onto her back before slowly kissing down over her neck and shoulders. Keeping my leg firmly wedged between her thighs, she thrust against my leg as I sucked one nipple into my mouth, lathing it with my tongue and feeling it pebble further.

Savannah tangled her fingers in my hair as I continued to suck at her breasts. Her moans and the feel of her soft body against mine made me crazy with need. I kissed down over her stomach to her hip. Leaving tiny nips along the way that I soothed with my tongue before I inhaled the scent of her arousal.

It was a scent that I would never tire of. Parting her legs, I leaned down and swiped my tongue against her crease, sucking each lip, feeling it swell in my mouth. Savannah's moans rang out as I teased her pussy and played it like the strings of a guitar. Her clit was begging for attention, and when I finally pressed the flat of my tongue against the aching bud, Savannah's body stiffened, and her hands tightened in my hair.

I continued to tongue her clit, sliding two fingers inside her wet warmth.

"Oh God, I'm gonna cum, fuck, I'm cumming," Savannah cried as her pussy soaked my face. Savannah's thighs tightened, and her pussy pulsed around my fingers.

I moved back up the bed to hover over my mate. Looking down at her, I pressed my lips against hers and tangled our tongues just as I felt Donte's cock penetrate me. Moaning, I pushed back against Donte, fucking him hard. Slipping my hand between mine and Savannah's body, I continued to press on her clit. Savannah lifted her legs and ground against my hand. Her cries mingled with mine.

My orgasm was on edge when I felt Savannah's hand snake between us. She pressed on my clit hard, stars floated behind my eyes, and I cried out just as Donte's roar filled the room, and his seed filled my pussy.

Slowly I floated back to reality and looked down at my mate, watching me with a smile.

"I love you," I said as I pressed a quick kiss to her lips. Donte rolled from my body and laid beside me. "I love you, Donte."

Donte's eyes widened, and a broad smile took over his face. "I love you too. I think I'm the luckiest man alive."

Savannah and I giggled. Being with Donte made us feel like the luckiest women alive.

"As much as I want to stay in bed all day and do this, we have to get up, we probably all need a shower, and we have to go to get our scans," Savannah said.

I sighed and nodded my head. I would've loved to stay in bed, but she was correct; there was so much for us to do.

# Chapter Seventeen

Donte

If someone had told me only six months earlier, I would be sitting in a hospital room with my two mates while one was giving birth and the other had just started labor; I would have laughed in their face. Yet that was my life. Savannah sat on a giant exercise ball, her contractions had only just started, and she was able to cope; that was what she said anyway. I suspected she was a little further along than she was letting on because she didn't want to miss out on seeing Sable give birth.

Sable, on the other hand, was just about screaming the hospital down in pain. They'd given her the gas, but it wasn't doing much. We'd asked for an epidural, but apparently, she was too close to giving birth for it to be effective. So, she had to push through.

"Fucking, Jesus, fucking Christ, this is the biggest baby I think to ever be born," Sable growled through gritted teeth.

I smirked. I couldn't help it. I felt terrible for Sable, she was in a lot of pain, but she was also hilarious to watch. She tried so hard to hold onto her alpha status and pretend she was tough, but I don't think there is a person alive that could go through childbirth without swearing at least once.

The Wild Claw Pack alphas stood guard at the door. They'd moved to the new pack land. Along with Maddox, the local carpenters team and some of the Wild Claw Pack who were builders, the houses were erected in no time and the pack was all moving in. It took only a month to get the majority of the homes built.

I loved getting to know them all. I'd been in to see Connell regularly, and we were getting constant updates from Kade about how he was doing. Apparently, Connell had been able to befriend Granger Redburn easily and get some of the information that was needed. Of course, that information had to be checked out. We all knew that it could be bullshit because Ettore was suspicious. Especially after the warlock team and the AJE authority shut down the Hunter Island Facility that Ettore was running.

"Oh god, I can feel it coming," Sable groaned. I focused my gaze on my mate as the nurse took her position between her legs.

"Sure is; I can see the head. I reckon one more big push, and you will have the head out," the nurse encouraged.

Sable ground her teeth and let out a cry as she bore down. I watched in a mixture of horror and astonishment as our baby's head appeared. Full of dark hair. Their face was pointed toward the bed, but it was only a matter of moments before they came screaming into the world.

"What have you got, Dad?" the nurse asked as she turned the baby over.

"A boy, baby, we have a boy," I said with a grin as I looked down into my son's face.

"Would you like to cut the cord?" I nodded and reached out for the scissors the nurse held out to me. Cutting through the cord where she pointed, I watched as my son was finally released into the world.

He laid on Sable's body, looking around. He was so alert. I leaned forward and kissed Sable on the side of the head.

"You did so well, baby," I said between kisses.

"Have you got a name for him?" the nurse asked.

I shook my head. "No, we name our children on the first full moon."

The nurse smiled and nodded, just as Savannah let out a groan. I quickly kissed Sable before leaving her side and going to my other mate.

"I think this baby is coming into the world sooner than I thought," Savannah grunted.

My eyes widened. "Like how soon."

"Like now," she groaned as she stood and quickly started to wrestle out of her underwear.

"Oh shit," the nurse said, pressing the buzzer beside the bed. Nurses and doctors came running into the room. "We've got another baby coming now."

Doctor Rankin, who we knew well, came into the room laughing. "Well, when you do it, you sure do it in style. Come on, girl, would you rather birth standing or on the couch?"

"I don't think we have time," Savannah cried wide-eyed as she thrust her hands between her legs.

Dr. Rankin kneeled on the ground, just in time to catch the baby as it came falling from Savannah. I wasn't sure if it was the shock or I'd completely lost my mind at that moment, but I couldn't stop laughing. Hysterical giggles fell from my lips.

"That had to be the best catch in history; you should've been a footy player," I said.

Dr. Rankin chuckled. "Plenty of practice. But have a look at what you've got."

I glanced down at the baby in Dr. Rankin's arms as the nurses wheeled in a second bed. "A girl. I have a son and a daughter," I cheered.

Once our daughter's cord was cut and Savannah was laid up on the bed, I went out into the waiting area full of people. Not just Wild Claw Pack, but Devil's Advocates and Savannah's family.

"Well, I can announce we have two very healthy babies," I said to everyone. "Sable gave birth to our son, and Savannah gave birth to our daughter."

A loud cheer went through the room. Everyone crowded me and said their congratulations. After that it was a sea of visitors taking turns to visit with Sable, Savannah and the babies. Each visitor kissed the babies and welcomed them into the world with a tiny blessing spoken over them. Even Savannah's family had accepted our son as one of their own. Our children had a huge family. One that would love them unconditionally and protect them with their very fiber.

Savannah

It had been almost four weeks since we'd given birth to the babies, and we were about to celebrate the full moon. This was something strange to me, yet somehow comforting. It was like an extra celebration of life. We'd all gathered on the Wild Claw Pack lands. They were terrific people, and I'd been so blessed to be welcomed into their life. The way they all strived to get to know Donte was excellent. I saw my mate finally free for the first time since knowing him. He didn't have that dark cloud that seemed to be hanging on around him.

Every day I spent with Sable was better than the last. I loved having her as a mate, and our children being born on the same day was an added bonus. I'd wondered throughout the pregnancy whether there would be a division of her child and mine, but it wasn't like that. The children were ours. It didn't matter if our daughter cried or our son; whoever was closest picked them up. There were times I breastfed our son, and Sable breastfed our daughter. It was just the way it went. And I loved it.

"All the food is ready and set out," I said as I looked at the vast array of food. My entire family was coming, which was why we'd decided to hold it on the pack lands. My family was immense. But also, all of the Devil's Advocates, Obsidian Mechanics, and half of the Rigby family would be in attendance too.

I couldn't believe how lucky I was. Our lives have been blessed in so many ways. Not just with Donte and me but being welcomed into the Devil's Advocates and the pack. I mean, the Wild Claw Pack could've rejected Donte. They could've turned their back or not bothered looking for him. But instead, they brought him in and loved him like he'd never been lost.

Sable wrapped her arm around my shoulder and kissed my cheek. "Finally, our babies will have a name."

"Yeah, baby boy and baby girl weren't so appealing," I snorted with a laugh.

Sable giggled and nodded her head.

"How does the ceremony work?" Iver asked as he came towards us.

"I suppose this is different for you," I said to Iver before turning to Sable. "Iver normally can tell us what the name of the babies are and what gender and species they are while pregnant."

Iver nodded his head and smiled. "I didn't ask with you because the creator told me that there is a ceremony."

Sable nodded. "That's right. In the Wild Claw Pack, there is. I don't know if this happens in other packs, but in ours, the children will be named on the first full moon after their birth. Usually, it falls around a month after the babies are born. The lead alpha, normally Connell, but will be Ward until Connell is out of prison, will say a blessing over the baby. Then with water from the pack lands stream that we believe was blessed by the angel that created the first wolf Nephilim, he will coat the baby's belly. Then when the full moon reaches its highest point, the name will form on their belly in the water."

I was amazed when Sable and the alphas explained to me about the ceremony, it sounded fascinating, and I love the idea of such tradition. Iver's eyes were wide as he listened. I couldn't wait for it to happen.

"That is amazing," Iver said. "Selene is the goddess of the moon. It is her that places her hand on the children."

It was Sable's turn to look shocked. "How do you know that?"

"The creator just told me."

Sable turned and called out for Ward, Herrick, and Fenris. When they came over, Sable pointed at Iver. "Tell them what you just told me."

"The goddess of the moon is Selene. She is the one that names your children. It is her that you all have derived your power."

The alphas looked at Iver with shock. "He's right," Anghus said from behind us.

"How do you know this?" Ward asked Iver.

"The creator told me. I was asking how the ceremony worked, and that was when I received the message."

Ward shook his head and chuckled. "If we didn't have proof before, we do now."

"Proof of what?" Anghus asked.

"That joining you and the rest of the Devil's Advocates were meant to be. The Nephilim that created the Wild Claw Pack was Mousaios, the child of Selene. It is said that Selene was raped by an angel and that was how Mousaios was conceived. As a result, Mousaios was sent to earth to create a better world. Mousaios was also the only female wolf Nephilim. The rest were all male. In human knowledge, she is known as the goddess of poetry and song because she would roam the pack lands and sing; her song was like that of a siren. However, it only attracted evil men. She would then kill them. Her writings have been handed down for centuries through our pack," Ward explained.

"Holy shit. That is amazing," Anghus gasped.

Ward nodded his head. "But want to know something even more amazing. In her writings, she talks about a time when rare supernaturals would lead the rest in a battle like nothing anyone had ever seen. And the leader of that battle?" Ward looked down at Iver before he glanced back at Anghus. "Is cthulu."

Anghus gasped and his whole face morphed into shock. "Am I able to read these writings?"

Ward smiled and nodded his head. "Sure. They can't leave the pack lands, but you are welcome to come and read them in our library."

"I'd love that. And if it is alright, I'd like to bring Arcadia; she is the record keeper for supernaturals."

Ward nodded again. "I've heard of Arcadia. That wouldn't be a problem."

"Thank you."

By the time the night fell, and the moon was high in the air, the group had a surge of excitement. Everyone was waiting with anticipation.

Knowing the story of Selene made the ceremony even that bit more special.

"We are about to start the ceremony if you would bring baby girl up to the front," Ward said as he laid his hand on my back.

I nodded and followed him to the front of the yard, where Donte and Sable were standing. I glanced up into the sky and saw that the moon was high.

"Strip the babies out of their suits, leave their diapers on. Their bellies just have to be bare," Ward explained. Sable and I stripped the babies out of their grow suits and held them tight to our bodies to prevent any chill.

"Thank you, everyone, for joining us for the naming ceremony of our two latest children. The moon is high, and the goddess Selene is ready to lay her blessings on the children." Ward stepped toward us and lifted the jug which held the blessed water. He dipped in a cloth, soaking it before resting it on our daughter's stomach and repeating the process on our son. Surprisingly the children didn't cry or squawk; they cooed happily as if they knew what was happening.

"These children, I pray, will have a long and prosperous life, as alphas of the Wild Claw Pack, but also of the Devil's Advocates and Adam's family. I ask that the goddess of the moon Selene come and pour her blessings upon the children and reveal to us their name," Ward said.

I stared at the baby girl's stomach and gasped as the moonlight hit the water. Slowly the water started to morph into letters before it formed a word.

"Selene has gifted the children powerful names. First, I present Myla, soldier of mercy," Ward said as he traced a sigil in the water and kissed my daughter's cheek before moving over to our son. "And Nakoa, warrior." Ward traced a different sigil on Nakoa's stomach before kissing his cheek.

"These children are born powerful, to rise up with the cthulu that is written about and prophesied. They will fight in his army and destroy all the evil against them," Ward announced.

All around us, a howl swept through the air as I watched in astonishment as the Wild Claw Pack stripped from their clothes and shifted into wolves of all shapes and colors. They took off at a run into the forest, howling and yipping. I smiled and looked over at Donte, who looked just as eager to join the pack.

"What are you waiting for? Get on in there and join your family," I said with a laugh.

Donte chuckled and quickly stripped out of his clothes before shifting and tearing off into the night.

"Myla and Nakoa, such beautiful babies," March said as he came over to where I stood. Hiro was perched on his hip and tucked his head against March's shoulder.

I kissed my brother's cheek and leaned into his hug. "Thank you. How are you doing?"

March sighed. "Some days are better than others. But the medication and therapy sessions are helping."

March had started therapy not long after Hiro was born. He was struggling with postpartum depression but also working with the knowledge that he couldn't have any more children. It had been hard on him. But with Asher's strength by his side, some anti-depressants, and therapy, I watched my little brother return to the person he once was.

"I can't believe how lucky I've gotten."

March shook his head. "There was no luck about it. This was all written in the stars. Or, in your case, little ones, the moon."

The end.

# Don't miss out!

Visit the website below and you can sign up to receive emails whenever S L Davies publishes a new book. There's no charge and no obligation.

https://books2read.com/r/B-A-NZRR-CHEBC

**BOOKS 2 READ**

Connecting independent readers to independent writers.

# Also by S L Davies

**Breeding Facility**
Memphis
Bacchus
Coltrane
Pax
Raiden
Nash


**Devil's Advocates**
Lynx
Israel
Jai
Jasper
Arley
Zion
Oakland


**KINK**
Freya
Tanquil

**Obsidian Mechanics**
Donte


**Onyx Rebels**
Onyx Rebels Prologue
Hawke


**Rigby Brothers**
Asher


**Schiavu**
Schiavu


**Standalone**
Sisters Revenge
Killer Love
Soldiers At War
Second Chances
Bunny
Caged

# About the Author

S L Davies is an Australian Author living in Country, Victoria. She is inspired by the world around her.

Read more at https://www.amazon.com/~/e/B0832T8F7Z.